Mrs. Rus

written by Ann-Marie Parker
illustrated by Jo Thapa

KAEDEN ❤ BOOKS™

Mrs. Rush-Around lived in a very big house. She had a dog, two cats, three mice, four rabbits, lots of children and a very big garden.

Mrs. Rush-Around was always busy.

There was always so much to do.

How was she going to get everything done?

So Mrs. Rush-Around came up with a great
idea. "I'll just have to do two things at once,"
she said. "Then I'll be able to finish
everything."

So that was what she did!

The next morning she had to bake a
chocolate cake for the twins' birthday.
"That's easy," she said. "I'll just bake the
cake while I make the cats' breakfast."

But the cat treats went into the chocolate cake. And she covered the cats' breakfast with chocolate icing.

Time to slow down, Mrs. Rush-Around!

But Mrs. Rush-Around didn't stop.
She had more work to do.

The dog was feeling sick. He had eaten the leftover breakfast and half a bag of dog biscuits.

"Don't worry," said Mrs. Rush-Around.
"I'll drop you off at the vet after I've taken
the children to school."

But she left the children at the vet and she
took the dog to school.

Time to slow down, Mrs. Rush-Around!

When she got home it was time to do the laundry. "Okay," said Mrs. Rush-Around, "I'll just do the laundry while I feed the tomato plants."

But she put the plant food in the washing machine and she put the laundry detergent on the plants.

Time to slow down, Mrs. Rush-Around!

But Mrs. Rush-Around didn't stop.

After the laundry it was time to mail her letters. "That's easy," said Mrs. Rush-Around. "I'll just mail the letters on the way to the dry cleaners."

So she put the clothes in the mailbox and handed the letters to the woman at the dry cleaners.

"Mrs. Rush-Around," called the woman in the dry cleaners. But it was too late, Mrs. Rush-Around was out the door and on her way home.

"Oh, what a busy morning," said
Mrs. Rush-Around, when she got home.
"I'll just rest my feet for a moment."

19

Just as she sat down in her favorite chair, the doorbell rang.

She opened the door and who did she see?

She saw her children with the vet and the teacher with the dog. The mailman was carrying her dirty clothes and the woman from the dry cleaners was holding her letters.

"It's time to slow down, Mrs. Rush-Around,"
they all said together.

"Oh, what a mess," laughed
Mrs. Rush-Around. "Tomorrow I promise
to slow down."

Everyone thought that was a great idea.